For Billy and Max

Library of Congress Cataloging in Publication Data   Arnosky, Jim.   Raccoons and ripe corn. Summary: Hungry raccoons feast at night in a field of ripe corn. 1. Raccoons—Food—Juvenile literature. 2. Raccoons—Juvenile literature. 3. Corn—Juvenile literature. [1. Raccoons] I. Title. QL737.C26A76   1987   599.74′443   87-4243   ISBN 0-688-10489-4

Raccoons
and
Ripe Corn

JIM ARNOSKY

A MULBERRY PAPERBACK BOOK
New York

It is autumn.
Leaves from trees near the edge of a farm sail over the cornfield.

The silk at the top
of the ears of corn
is turning brown.

The corn is plump and ripe.

At night, a mother raccoon
and her almost-grown kits
sneak into the cornfield.

The raccoons walk
between the rows of corn.

They climb the tall stalks

and pull the ears down
to the ground.

They peel away the green husks
that cover the yellow kernels.

All night long
the raccoons feast on corn.

They pull down more corn
than they can eat.

At sunrise, the raccoons hurry back
into the woods.

Wind whistling through the trees
sends autumn leaves sailing out
over the field of ripe corn.